Mapping the Interior

ALSO BY STEPHEN GRAHAM JONES

MAPPING
—— THE ——
INTERIOR

STEPHEN GRAHAM JONES

A TOM DOHERTY ASSOCIATES BOOK

NEW YORK

MAPPING THE INTERIOR

Cover art by Greg Ruth
Cover design by Christine Foltzer

Edited by Ellen Datlow

A Tor.com Book
Published by Tom Doherty Associates
175 Fifth Avenue
New York, NY 10010

www.tor.com

Tor® is a registered trademark of
Macmillan Publishing Group, LLC.

ISBN 978-0-7653-9509-2 (ebook)
ISBN 978-0-7653-9510-8 (trade paperback)

First Edition: June 2017

For Kelly O'Connor: thank you

Mapping the Interior

I was twelve the first time I saw my dead father cross from the kitchen doorway to the hall that led back to the utility room.

It was 2:49 in the morning, as near as I could reconstruct.

I was standing alongside the dusty curtain pulled across the front window of the living room. I wasn't standing there on purpose. I was in only my underwear. No lights were on.

My best guess is that, moments before, I'd been looking out the front window, into all the scrub and nothing spread out in front of our house. The reason for thinking that was I had the taste of dust in the back of my throat, and the window had a fine coat of that dust on it. Probably. I'd breathed it in through my nose, because sleepwalkers are goal oriented, not concerned with details or consequences.

If sleepwalkers cared about that kind of stuff, I'd have at least had my gym shorts on, and, if I was in fact trying to see something outside, then my glasses, too.

To sleepwalk is to be inhabited, yes, but not by something else, so much. What you're inhabited by, what's kicking one foot in front of the other, it's yourself. It doesn't make sense, but I don't think it's under any real compulsion to, finally. If anything, being inhabited by yourself like that, what it tells you is that there's a real you squirming down inside you, trying all through the day to pull up to the surface, look out. But it can only get that done when your defenses are down. When you're sleeping.

The following morning—this was my usual procedure, after a night of shuffling around dead to the world—would find me out in the sun, poring over the stunted grass and packed dirt for eighty or a hundred feet past the front window. Mom would be at work, and my little brother, Dino, would be glued to one of his cartoons, so there would be nobody there to call out from the porch, ask me what was I doing.

If I'd had to answer, I'd have said I was looking for whatever it was I'd been looking for last night. My hope was that my waking self had cued on some regularity to the packed dirt's contour, or registered a dull old pull tab that was actually the lifting ring for a dry old plywood door that opened onto . . . what? I didn't care. Just something. Anything. An old stash of fireworks, a buried body, a capped-off well; it didn't matter.

The day I found something, that would mean that my nighttime ramblings, they had purpose.

Otherwise, I was just broken, right? Otherwise, I was just a toy waking up in the night, bumping into walls.

That next morning, though, my probing fingers turned up nothing of any consequence. Just the usual trash—little glass bottles, a few bolts with nuts and washers rusted to the thread, part of a dog collar, either the half-buried wheel of a car long gone or the still-at-tached wheel of a car now buried upside down.

I wanted the latter, of course, but, to allow that possibility, I had to resist digging around the edges of that wheel.

When I looked back to the front window of our modular house, I half-expected to see the shape of my dead father again, standing in the window. Watching me.

The window was just the window, the curtain drawn like Mom said, to keep the heat out.

Still, I watched it.

How I'd know it was him from a house length out, it wasn't that I would recognize his face or his build. He'd died when I was four and nearly dying from pneumonia myself, when Dino was one and staying with an aunt so he couldn't catch pneumonia, when Mom was still working just one shift. All I had to go on as far as how he looked, it was pretty much just snapshots and a blurry memory or two.

No, the way I'd recognized him the night before, when

he was walking from the kitchen doorway back to the utility room, it was his silhouette. There were spikes coming out from his lower back, and the tops of his calves bulged out in an unnatural way, and his head was top-heavy and kind of undulating, so he was going to have to duck to make it into the utility room.

But—for all he was wearing, he was absolutely silent. Zero rustling, like you can usually hear with a fancy-dancer, when they're all set to go, or have just finished.

Thing was? My father never danced. He didn't go to the pow-wows to compete for cash. One of the few things I remember about him, it's that he didn't call the traditionals down at the town pump or the IGA "throwbacks," like I'd heard. His words always got scrambled in his mouth—Dino's got that too—so that what he came out with, it was "fallback."

My father was neither a throwback nor a fallback. He didn't speak the language, didn't know the stories, and didn't care that he didn't. Once or twice a year, he'd sign on to fight whatever fire was happening, but it wasn't to protect any ancestral land. It was because when you signed on, they issued you these green wool pants. He'd sell those to the hunters, come fall. Once a year, Mom told me, he'd usually walk home in his boxers, with a twenty folded small in his hand so none of the reservation dogs would nose it away.

That's my dad, as I know him.

But in the year or two after he either drowned or was drowned—there's stories both ways, and they each make sense—when we were still on the reservation, when his sisters would still watch us some days, they'd tell us about Dad when he was our age and his eyes were still big with dreams.

He'd been really into bows and arrows and headbands, they said, the toy ones from the trading post. I imagine that when you grow up in a cowboy place, then you're all into saddles and boots and ropes. When you grow up in Indian country, the TV tells you how to be Indian. And it starts with bows and arrows and headbands. They're the exciting part of your heritage. They're also the thing you can always find at the gift shop.

Back then, Dad would always be in the stands at the pow-wows, his sisters told me—well, me and Dino, but Dino was one and two, so I think the stories just skidded right past him, pretty much.

As for me, I really keyed on that, on my dad watching those dancers with every last bit of his attention, his headband strapped tight over his hair. Like he was trying to soak all this in, so it could fill him up. So he could *be* that.

Who wouldn't want to step into a fancydancer outfit? It would be the obvious next step.

The bustles, the armbands, the beadwork, the cool knee-high moccasins—and the facepaint. It makes you look like the assassin-aliens in space movies. With your face black and white like that, you automatically slit your eyes like a gunfighter, like you're staring America down across the centuries.

I can see my dad slitting his eyes in the bleachers like that all those years ago. What he's doing, it's pretending. What he's doing, it's waiting.

"He was going to be the best dancer of us all, once he straightened back up again," one of his sisters had told me. She wasn't a dancer herself, but, playing it again in my head, I think she was talking about all the Indians on the whole reservation, maybe even on the whole pow-wow circuit. I think she was saying that if my dad would have just applied the same energy and forethought to his regalia and his routine as he did to what trouble there was to get in once the sun came down, there would have been no stopping him.

That's how you talk about dead people, though, especially dead Indians. It's all about squandered potential, not actual accomplishments.

My father, my dad, he *could* have been the best fancy-dancer of us all.

And that's how I recognized him that first night, crossing from the living room through the kitchen.

His boots, his bustle. His fancydancer outline.

In death, he had become what he never could in life.

And now he was back.

Or, he had been for a few steps.

My heart pounded in my chest with what I wanted to call fear but what I know now was actually hope.

~

Our house, like I said, it was modular.

You can leave the reservation, but your income level will still land you in a reservation house, won't it? I'd heard my mom say this on the phone once, and it had stuck to the inside of my head in a way I knew I was going to be looking over at that part of the inside of my skull for the rest of my life, probably.

I read once that a baby elephant doesn't have the digestive enzymes it needs to live, but it can get them—and does—by eating its mother's dung.

That's an old Indian story, right there.

Anyway, the house we were renting, it was 1140 square feet. I knew that from a sticker on the backside of the cabinet under the sink.

Square feet don't tell you anything, though.

For delivery purposes, our house was almost twenty feet wide and nearly three times as long, about. My tape-measuring involved Dino holding it steady for me every twelve feet, though, a red popsicle melting down his left fist, so there could have been some missing inches.

Twenty feet wide sounds like a trailer house, I know, which we'd also lived in, but the difference in a trailer house and modular one, it's that a modular house, it gets delivered and it stays there, more or less, while a trailer house keeps its wheels and the tongue it gets pulled with, so it can still roam if need be. They've both got skirts that never last the winter, though, and the sidings are pretty much the same, and if you end up with one of each, you can kind of rub them together like puffy Cheetos and make a bigger, more complicated house.

I say all this because, the week after I saw my dad in the house, I scoured every single inch of those 1140 square feet for evidence of his having walked through.

What I wanted was a single lost bead, just one stray, bright-blue feather. Even a waxy smear on a doorjamb, that could be where he'd touched after he'd wiped an itch on his cheek.

He was back watching us, I knew.

It made me sterner with Dino, to prove the good big brother I was being in Dad's absence. How I was picking up the slack.

It also made me ask Mom questions about Dad, on as much of the sly as I could manage. What was the first car he had? What was the last? Where did she meet him? What was he doing? Did he name me, or did she? What was the best fight he was ever in? How much could he lift if he had to?

They're questions a nine-year-old would ask, I know, not a sixth-grader, but I think when you're talking about your dad, you kind of go back in years—the more you become a kid, the more he gets to be the dad, right?

So, we ate crunchy fish sticks over the game shows of dinner, and Mom shrugged and chewed and told me some stories. Not the ones I was ever asking for but ones she remembered from when he was a senior and she was a sophomore. How Dad had come to school with his whole head shaved once, to prove something to a teacher. Or how one time she saw him standing by the lake and throwing a trash bag of shoes into the water, shoe by shoe.

He hadn't made it through to graduation—who ever does?—but he'd been there all the same, and he'd clapped louder than anybody, and hooted for every person who crossed the stage, and Mom thought that was probably either the first or the second weekend he ever had to spend in jail.

When he died, they didn't find him right off. The tribal cops, I mean. But everybody knew where he was. Probably some kids from my own class had even snuck out to see him, dragged by their older brothers and sisters, meaning they knew my dad was dead before I did.

Was it because a truck he was driving had thrown a rod he couldn't afford to pay for, or was it because he was drinking and stumbled, and couldn't get back up?

There were stories both ways, and Mom told us that either being true wouldn't make him alive again, and that—she only said this when she was down—we were maybe better off anyway. We never would have left otherwise.

Now I was going to a school with a higher graduation rate, and there weren't as many fights.

Also, there weren't dogs smiling at us around every corner, or faces we knew in cars driving by, or the snow coming off the mountains the same way, but it was supposed to all be worth it in the end.

And, as near as I could tell, there were no beads or feathers or facepaint anywhere in the house. No proof of Dad having walked through. I even checked the vacuum cleaner bag, even though we hardly ever used the vacuum because the smell from the belts always made us have to eat our fish sticks outside.

That didn't mean I was done looking, though.

If I couldn't find any trace of him, then maybe I could reconstruct what he'd been *doing*.

Over and over, and slower and slower, I walked what

I'd seen of his path from the kitchen to the utility room. Maybe fourteen feet—a little longer than the tape measure would go. I looked at every chair back and coffee-table edge and wall he could have brushed by, that he could have touched with his fingertips the way I imagine the dead touch solid things: with wonder.

Then I backtracked, figured he must have crossed the living room before crossing the kitchen, right? Which meant he'd walked right behind me when I was standing there asleep, looking out into the driveway—*meaning* that, maybe, my sleeping self had heard his ghost truck pull up out there. That truck with the thrown rod, the truck he'd killed, that had maybe killed him. I'd heard it and risen to watch him walk up, but, asleep, I'd been too slow. He'd probably been coming through the front door right as I was parting the curtain, and then had been walking behind me when my sleeping eyes were trying to see out into the dark. It was pure luck that I'd sensed motion in my peripheral vision, and that flurry of movement had shaken me awake, pulled my head around to barely catch him slipping out the kitchen.

To the utility room.

Mom caught me in there when she got home from work.

I had her roll of duct tape, was tearing some out, then pressing it to every surface in there, trying to lift something that would prove I'd seen what I'd seen.

"Junior?" she said, standing in the doorway.

I didn't try to explain. What I asked her instead was were there any secret compartments in here, or any old photo albums, or maybe a box of old leftover clothes, something like that?

She didn't answer, just watched me some more.

"What have you been reading?" she asked.

Our questions were going right past each other, as usual.

Another effect Dad being back was having was that I was less patient with Mom now. Quicker to dismiss her. I mean, sure, that could be part of being twelve. But I think it was my way of siding with my dad, too.

I don't claim to be smart or good or right or any of that.

My name's "Junior," after all. I'm my father's son.

~

When two thirty rolled around that morning, I was rooted to the exact same spot by the front window. I was even still wearing the exact same underwear. The only difference was that I had my glasses on now. I hoped they wouldn't mess everything up.

What I'd also done, just on the chance this was key,

was deadfoot it into the living room. It was something I'd learned at my new school, listening in: if both your feet fell asleep and you walked around anyway, you could accidentally step into some other world. I figured that's maybe what had happened to me the night before—my feet had been asleep but I'd walked on them anyway, into some other ... not plane, I don't think, but like a shade over, or deeper, or shallower, where I could see more than I could otherwise.

The difference, it was that I wasn't asleep. To try to make up for it, I'd snaked one of Dino's jump ropes—they were supposed to teach him to count, if anything ever would—and pythoned it tight around my thighs until the beds of my toenails had started to darken.

My concern now was that, by being early so as to be sure not to miss anything, I was also insuring that my feet would be awake by 2:49, and I'd be standing in the same waking level or depth I was standing in every other day.

At 2:43, the skin on the outside of each of my feet started to tingle and pinprick. I hotfooted it back and forth without thinking, then just stood there looking down at what was happening. Circulation. It was ruining everything.

I could gamble that it didn't matter what my blood was doing, and whether that blood was somehow connected to my brain in a way that nudged my vision over just enough, or . . . I did it, I sat down right there and tied my legs off one more time, tighter than before, and pulled the rope between my teeth instead of knotting it like last time.

This time, it hurt. I think it was because all the blood that had just got to go back where it was supposed to have been, it had only been starting to make the turn, suck back up to my heart, but now I was shutting it off again. It felt like my feet were balloons. When they weren't supposed to feel like anything.

I pulled tighter, closing my eyes, leaning back to do it, and then jerked forward when our dog Chuckhead brushed my bare back with his mangy, matted coat.

An instant after that, I remembered that Chuckhead hadn't come with us down here. He was living on the streets now, was trying to put on fat for winter, or else becoming fat for one of the bigger dogs.

Meaning?

I twisted around, letting the jump rope sling past my mouth, the handle taking a chunk of lipmeat with it, but I was alone. It wasn't the air conditioner or the fan, either. Mom kept the fan in her room mostly, and the air conditioner parasited onto the back window behind the TV was rusted shut.

I stood, forgetting I was supposed to be watching for some wavery version of headlights in front of the house.

Had it been a feather that brushed the skin of my back? The ermine cuff of a fancy moccasin? The lightest brush of a porcupine quill from a bustle?

Had my dad reached down with his fingertips to touch the back of his oldest son, because that was the most he could do?

I reached my hand as far around as I could.

Another thing I'd learned at school, it was "canteen kiss." It's when you drink after a girl you like, or she drinks after you.

This was like that, I guess.

If my dad had touched me, then there was some kind of countdown where I could touch where he'd touched, and it would matter.

It was two fifty. Then it was three. I had school the next morning.

I policed my area, being sure there was no evidence of my nocturnal activities—no explanation would cover me out here, mostly naked with a jump rope and a prayer—and walked the uncreaky parts of the floor back to my room, stopping to check on Dino for good measure.

He was spasming in his bed.

It wasn't the first time.

Mom swore she'd not had a drop of anything while carrying him, but still, and lately more and worse, he was kind of . . . It was like there was something in his head not quite making a complete connection. Like the way he wasn't learning his numbers or his letters when, by the third grade, he definitely should have. The school had him on some special learning plan already, but there was talk of special classes now, and special teachers that talk so soft and nice it's terrifying, like they're about to eat you.

At the bus stop, if I didn't stop it, the other kids would push him back and forth between them like playing pinball. And Dino didn't mind. He liked being part of the game, I think.

The last month or two, though, he'd started zoning out in the middle of meals, or while watching a game show, or just while standing looking out a window.

And now this.

"Mom," I called out, just loud enough to wake her, not loud enough that she'd hurt herself trying to crash down the hall, "Dino's having another seizure."

This would be his fifth or sixth. That we knew about.

By the time Mom got there with the warm rag she was sure helped, I had the leg of one of Dino's superhero action figures between his teeth. In the Western movies, they always use a belt or a wallet in the mouth. It's never for a seizure, it's usually for a bullet, but the principle's the same, I figured.

After a few minutes of it, Dino settled down.

I stood to go to bed.

"What were you doing up with that?" Mom said.

I looked down to the jump rope evidently still hanging around my neck.

"Water," I lied, like that was any kind of explanation, and then made good on that lie, felt my way to the sink.

On the way back across the linoleum of the kitchen, my bare foot kicked something that rocketed away. Something light and plastic and round.

My heart registered it the moment it hit the wall under the table, and then my hands reacted just about the exact instant it tapped against the roulette wheel of the heater vent in the floor.

My mouth named it while it was still falling down that ductwork: "Bead."

One single bead.

It was as big as the whole rest of the world.

~

After school, I held Dino's hand as soon as the bus pulled far enough away. If anybody saw, it wouldn't help his cause any, I didn't think. Probably not mine either, but I at least had the idea—mostly from action movies—that I could go wolverine, fight my way out of any dogpile of bodies.

This is something all Indians think, I think: that, yeah, we got colonized, yeah, we got all our lands stolen, yeah yeah yeah, all that usual stuff. But still, inside us, hiding—no, hibernating, waiting, curled up, is some Crazy Horse kind of fighter. Some killer who's smart and wily and wears a secret medicine shirt that actually works.

Just, if you say this to anybody, you kill that Crazy Horse you're hiding inside.

So, you walk around with this knowledge that he's there if you ever need him.

But, also, you try not to need him. You wait till the bus is a plume of dust before taking your little brother's hand in yours while you both walk past the neighbor's house. It's a ramshackle affair that might have been a tack shed originally, or maybe a camper with the wheels buried. There's chainlink all around the property, and that's usually high enough to keep his four dogs in. Dino walking in his jerky way, though, that activates whatever predator instincts those dogs still have, and they come at the chainlink hard, sometimes even bloody their face on it.

Me holding his hand, it was keeping his jerkiness under wraps, so the dogs just barked, didn't gear down into killer-snarl mode.

Again, we made it, and, to prove to Dino that we're not complete wimps, right at the end of the chainlink, I started making a hurt-rabbit sound in my throat, so that my mouth didn't move—so that anybody in that ramshackle tar-paper house with the three galvanized chimneys wouldn't see that I'm doing anything.

But the dogs knew.

They exploded against the fence but it was taller at the corner, from the remains of what had probably been a chicken coop back in 1910, and that was all they could do: bark. If they knew to double back, they could have cleared the fence, hamstrung us halfway to our porch, have a midafternoon kidmeat feast. But dogs are stupid.

Anyway, it was Mom who hamstrung us.

She was waiting, wasn't at work.

She ran out to scoop us up, was enough of a surprise in the middle of the day that I had to swallow that hurt-rabbit sound and kind of go limp, let her pack us into the back seat of our big heavy car.

What happened, she explained, driving and smoking, it was that in the breakroom at her work, one of the other mom's kids had turned up sick at school, so he was at work with her, was wrapped in a blanket watching cartoons. The first thing this meant was Mom couldn't catch the last fifteen minutes of the soap opera she claimed not to care about, really. The second thing this meant was that, tapping ashes into the big brass ashtray of the breakroom, she was now watching a whole new set of commercials. Ones targeted at an audience into robots and di-nosaurs and fighter planes, not vitamins and hygiene and vacations.

What *this* meant was that she ended up tracking the movements of an action figure on screen, and that cued up last night for her, Dino's seizure in his bed, and then she was leaving her cigarette curling up smoke from the ashtray. She didn't even clock out, just raced straight home to wait on the porch for us.

Because she knew.

I'm not saying she was the perfect mom, but she would always pick us over whatever else there was. When we left the reservation, it was for me and Dino. Not for her. Unlike Dad, she wasn't still living her high school years five years after high school. But she did have her own sisters, and one brother still alive, and aunts and uncles and cousins and the rest, kind of like a net she could fall back into, if she ever needed them all.

But she cashed all that in. Because, she said, she didn't want either one of us drowning in water we didn't have to drown in, someday.

Only, now, one of us, he was malfunctioning. And she was the only one who could run him to the doctor in the middle of the day.

We had to sit in the waiting room nearly until dinner, but the emergency room finally took Dino back to x-ray his third-grade body. Not for whatever misfire was making him zone out and seize up—that had to be in his head—but for the superhero foot Mom knew would be there. In the breakroom at work, she'd flashed on the action figure I'd had him bite down on. It was lying beside him in bed once he calmed down. And it had been missing one red boot.

In the breakroom, I spent all three of the dollars Mom had left, ate two honey buns and one hot chocolate from the coffee machine. I sprinkled grainy sugar from the coffee table onto the second honey bun, then, hours later, walking across the parking lot holding Mom's hand, I threw up right in front of a parked ambulance and couldn't understand what was going on.

Mom tried to pull me away from the vomit—puley honey-bun paste, runneled through with dark chocolate veins—but I pulled back, studied it, trying to make a deal: *I* would throw up that superhero boot for Dino. Please. It was my fault, anyway.

That's not how the world works.

Dino was supposed to just keep eating like normal and wait to find that piece of plastic in the toilet. We didn't have to watch for it, though. We could, the doctor had said, but really, the sign that it had hung up somewhere, it would be Dino's appetite fading.

Except—what if his appetite started to go away because of whatever was happening in his head, to keep him from learning his numbers?

Mom was out of cigarettes, so she held on to the steering wheel with both hands and didn't look into the back seat, even with the mirror.

After lights out, still trying to make deals, I snuck Dino's one-footed superhero from his dresser, walked it into the kitchen and pried the vent up, dropped it down into that darkness, and then I tried to wait up for Dad, crossing the kitchen again, but fell asleep in the corner under the table and didn't wake until Mom draped a blanket over me in the morning.

~

The whole next week was nothing. Dino kept eating as much as ever, Mom got another carton of cigarettes, and I started digging up what I told myself wasn't a car from the front pasture, but a truck. *The* truck. Because ghosts need anchors in the physical, living world, don't they? What might have happened was that, up on the reservation, Dad runs a truck too hard, throws a rod, so that truck gets left behind. But someone else picks it up, drags it down here with plans of using it for a parts truck, or maybe they have an engine from a car that'll mate with the transmission.

What happens instead is that the truck gets left behind, and a landlord wants the place to look clean, so he scoops a hole in the ground with a tractor, then nudges that truck over in the hole, such that only one tire is sticking up, like the last hand of a drowning person. Give the sun and snow a couple years at that tire, though, and it's down to steel belts, then nothing. Just a rusted old rim some stupid kid can bark his shin against one day and then remember later, once the dead start walking.

I dug for the whole afternoon, and what I had convinced myself was an axle housing spearing out from that rusted wheel, it turned out to be a pipe welded to it, with a single chainlink tacked to the top of the pipe buried twelve feet behind me. I'd seen a link of chain tacked to a pipe like that before, at my old school. This was someone's old tetherball pole.

I stood it up. It rocked back and forth, settled, like waiting for what was next.

I had no idea what was next.

I looked to the house, to make sure Dino wasn't sneaking off the porch, and the curtain in the window was just falling back into place.

I went cold inside.

Mom was at work.

I took a single step backward, just instinct, and then I was running for the porch and then up the front of the porch, not the steps, and through the door, into the darkness inside.

Dino was seizing in front of his favorite cartoon, and—I remember this as clear as anything in my life—getting across the living room to him, even though it was only ten feet, it was all slow motion, it was like the carpet was tall or I was small, and I was having to wade through, fight my way over, reach ahead because this was all taking so long.

There was spittle frothed all on Dino's lips and his eyes were mostly back to the whites, and his fingers were going past double-jointed, his elbows pulling in, his pants hot with pee.

I forced my finger between his teeth, gave him that to bite on, and held him until the shaking stopped.

He came back in stages, like usual. By the end of it he was watching the next cartoon, hadn't even realized yet that his pants were wet, I don't think.

"Hey, man," I said. "You see what I found out there?"

He looked over to me like just realizing I was there.

"Out where?" he said.

I tilted my head out front.

He looked back to his cartoon, like being sure this was a moment in the story he could walk away from, and then he stood with his bag of chips, and—this was what I was testing—he didn't go to the window to look out front.

He went to the front door, hauled it open, studied the pasture through the storm door.

"It's a flagpole," I told him.

By the time Mom made it home, we had a home-drawn pirate flag up there in the wind, more or less. Because we didn't have enough black marker to make the pale yellow towel from the bathroom look scary, we'd used one of Mom's last two black dish towels. The face and bones were masking tape.

I thought we were going to get swatted, but instead, we ate sloppy joes on the porch and watched the pirate flag whip in the wind and finally break free of its knot, lift into the sky, come down on the wrong side of the neighbor's chainlink.

The dogs were on it right when it touched down. It probably tasted like a hundred and fifty dinners all at once.

"Hated that towel anyways," Mom said, and leaned back in her chair, blew smoke up into the dusk for a long time, and for the first time, I think, I was happy to be living right where we were.

The feeling didn't last.

~

That night—I want to say it was a dream, but I've never

remembered my dreams. Or maybe I walk through them.

Nothing happened. That I knew of.

I just slept even though I hadn't meant to, and woke in my bed, my feet not dirty or anything.

If Dino seizured in the night, he didn't bite his tongue or hurt himself.

Everything was so good, really, that I figured it kind of compelled me to keep my end of a deal I was only just now suspecting.

"Dad's back," I said over cereal, through the hustle and bustle and cussing of a weekday before school.

Mom was walking through the kitchen, on the way to the utility room, for Dino's other pair of pants. She took maybe three more steps and then she stopped, like re-listening in her head, and then she looked back to me.

"Say what?" she said.

"Dad," I said over my next, intentionally big, slurping bite. No eye contact.

Mom looked into the living room, like to be sure Dino had cartoons tuned in, not us.

"I don't know what you're talking about, Juney," she said.

I hated her calling me that.

I plunged my spoon into the bowl again.

"I saw him the other night," I said, shrugging like this was no big. "He's different now. Better."

"You saw him where?" Mom said, giving me her full attention now.

What she was thinking, I know, was the neighbors just had someone get processed out of lockup, and now they were standing out at the fence, watching the little boys who had moved in next door.

"Right here," I said, nodding to the kitchen. "He was going back to the utility room."

Mom just stared at me some more.

"Your father never did laundry," she finally said. "I don't think he would come back from the afterlife to run a load of whites."

In the living room the cartoon swelled and crashed, and we both listened underneath it for the heel of a foot spasming into the carpet.

Dino was okay, though. Sucking on a yogurt.

"He's a fancydancer now," I said. "You should see him."

Mom, even though there was never time for this in the morning, sat down across from me, skated both her hands across to hold the one of mine that was there.

"That's why you were asking about him," she said.

"He's my dad," I told her.

"You look like him," she said back. "I never tell you because I don't want to make you sad. But I remember him from elementary. If we were back home, everybody would be saying it."

This made my eyes hot. I looked away, took my hand back.

"He's coming back to help make Dino better," I said.

Mom wouldn't look away from my face.

"How would he find us, all the way down here?" she said, her voice like she was letting me down soft, here.

"We're his family," I said.

Mom nodded, looked past me, into the living room, and I realized then that she didn't miss him like I did.

It was why he'd shown himself to me, not her. It was why that bead had hidden itself in the ducts under the house, not stuck around for her to—

And then, all at once, like crashing over me, it hit me: I'd scoured every inch of every room of the *house*, sure. I'd even drawn our floor plan out, reducing the inches to millimeters on my ruler as best I could, to make sure there weren't any hidden rooms, any closets that had been boarded over by some past renter.

It was all there in my science notebook.

And, while I'd looked out in the pasture for evidence—only finding a ceremonially buried tetherball pole and the other usual trash of people having lived here once—I hadn't taken into account the most likely place a person who was dead might want to live, to be close to his family: *under* the house.

We were up on cinderblock pylon things, not settled

onto a concrete foundation. It was why the landlord had come over our first winter: to crawl down there, rewrap the pipes that had no other insulation. He said the varmints would chew it off again in a year or two, but we'd be good for the cold. And we had been, mostly.

"What?" Mom said, seeing some version of all this wash over my face, I guess.

"The bus," I said, rising with my bowl.

She took it from me, studied me for a moment too long, then flicked her head to the outside world, meaning *go, school already,* and like that, me and Dino were hand in hand down the rut-road to the bus stop, the dogs pacing us on the other side of the chainlink.

This time, when the kid from my PE nudged Dino over into a kid I didn't know, trying to get the game started, instead of my usual repositioning, my usual guiding Dino over to my other side, I lit into this kid without even saying anything first.

The bus driver had to pull me off. The kid was going to need a note for PE today. Maybe all week.

I hadn't even heard the air brakes hiss to a stop behind us.

Dino was just watching me, standing there with my chest heaving, tears coming all down my face.

"I've got him," the bus driver said, his hand to Dino's shoulder, and I nodded thank-you, was already running back along the chainlink, scraping my fingers over the rough wire the whole way, the dogs rising to the top of the fence again and again, snapping and snarling.

I ran faster, more headlong, and was just to the side of the house when the front door opened.

Our car started on the third try for Mom, and she didn't know she should have been looking behind the house for me. I was at school. It was just another day.

You look like him, she'd told me.

I could see him back home, too, just like this. My dad, at my age. Hiding behind my grandma's house, his face wet, the mountains opening up behind him.

But I could also see him standing from that, taller and taller, his shadow feathered and already moving like a dance.

The reason he was only showing up now to help Dino, it was that it had taken him a long time to walk all the way down here.

"I won't let them hurt Dino," I said into the side of the house, but really, I was trying to make sure he could hear me through the windblown cracks in the skirt.

Inside, the cartoon in the living room was still playing.

I sat down on the propane tank and ate my lunch three hours early and watched the skirt of the house for a response. For a finger reaching through. For an eye, watching out. For an older version of me, here to save us.

~

You could pull the skirt of the house out easy, I found. It was just tin or aluminum or something, corrugated like cardboard, but it would flap back into place as soon as you let go. So, I went out to the tetherball pole, leaned it over like pulling a flag down, and rolled it in about a thousand switchback arcs to the house.

Then it was just a matter of guiding the top of the pole in through a crack and working the wheel so the pole could hold the flap open.

That it worked so perfect told me I was on the right path.

But I still couldn't go in.

He was my dad, yeah. But he was also dead.

I walked back and forth in front of the house. I looked as deep into the dark as I could without crossing the threshold.

I squatted there and said, quiet because ghosts hear everything anyway, "Dad?"

I bet every Indian kid who's lost a dad, he does this at some point. I don't know why it's special to Indians. But I think it is.

He didn't say anything back at first, but when he did, I wasn't sure if it was in my ear or in my head. Either way, it was like he was using my own voice to do it.

It wasn't my name he said, or Mom's, or Dino's, or even hello.

What he said, what I heard, it was *Look*.

It made an instant lump in my throat. I fell back, sat in the dirt, the muscles close to all my bones grabbing tighter on to the bone.

Look.

I leaned forward, thought that was what he meant, but then a rustle behind me pulled my head around.

The rustle wasn't the top cuffs of boots brushing into each other, and it wasn't a rattle being held deep in a hand, to hush it.

It was a dog, standing there, big strings of saliva coming down from its mouth.

It was halfway between me and where the tetherball pole had been buried. The reason it was just standing there, it was that it was probably questioning what it had done to deserve a gift like this. It was waiting for me to just be a mirage, a dream.

One that was making it slobber all the way down to the ground.

It had gone to that dug-up hole first, I think. For the new smells. Maybe that was part of the route it took into the pasture every day, when it jumped the fence, went on patrol, or hunting, or whatever it did.

But now here was me. I didn't even make sense. At first.

When I did, the dog's haunches bunched and dirt shot up behind it and its mouth opened to tell me what all it was going to do to me.

I squeaked a sound of pure fear, twisted around, and kicked through the skirt, into the darkness under the house, and only just managed to guide the tetherball pole out at the last instant, so the flap could shut the dog out.

It clawed at the base of the skirt and barked and snarled enough that the rest of the dogs finally came over the fence for whatever this was.

It was me.

I was crying and snuffling and hugging myself, having to keep my head low so it wouldn't collect all the webs spun under the floor of the living room—which, if this was the underside of the *living* room, then what did that make it, right?

I wouldn't say it out loud, even in my head.

~

I'd seen coyotes go after a rabbit, when they didn't have anything better to kill. They don't just dig a bit and give up, they excavate until they find a beating heart.

I was that rabbit, now.

The neighbor dogs, they'd been waiting for this ever since we moved in. The only thing that was saving me was that dogs only know to push, not to pull, and the one flap of the skirt that was loose, it overlapped a solid flap, so it would only push in for a car bumper someday.

Not that the dogs weren't trying.

That just scraped my nerves raw, though, which isn't permanent damage. What would be more permanent was when the other three caught onto what the yellowy-white one was already doing: reaching down with one big paddle of a paw, to dig under.

As big as these dogs were, and as sharp as the bottom of the skirt would be, they were going to have to really tunnel. But I trusted that they hated me enough to do just that. The prize would be worth the work.

I swallowed and the sound was loud in my ears.

My eyes had adjusted some now. Enough that the sunlight edging in through the cracks and seams in the skirt showed shapes, anyway.

I'd imagined it would smell like an animal den in here, that it would be moist and sticky.

It was just dry and dead.

I beat the side of my fist on the bottom of the living room, even though I'd seen my mom leave already. Moms are capable of a lot, I knew. I didn't put it past her to hear me needing help somehow and shrike across the thirteen miles from her work, tear into this pack with her bare hands.

What I got back, instead of an answering knock or a footstep, was a faceful of fine dust I was too slow to close my eyes against.

And then something was on my hand, something with feet. I panicked back into a strut or a pipe, shaking my whole arm like it was on fire, and a moth batted into my face. I registered what it was right away but still flinched back all the same, into that same strut or pipe or whatever, nearly knocking myself senseless.

This reinvigorated the dogs.

I didn't have to act like a hurt rabbit for them anymore. It wasn't an act anymore, I mean.

Now each time the yellowy-white paw stabbed down under the skirt for more dirt, it was like it was reaching down out of the sun.

Every few scoops, the paw would be replaced by a nose, breathing my fear in.

I pushed as far away as possible. I wasn't exactly thinking rationally. All I knew, I guess, it's that the more distance between me and them, the longer it might take them to find me.

If you can delay pain, you delay it, don't you? Even when it's inevitable. Especially when there's teeth involved.

The farthest I could get was right under Mom's bedroom.

The whole way there, it was just dirt and the old

dead weeds and grass that must have been live weeds and grass when this house got delivered here. They'd turned into mummies of themselves, mummies that crumbled into less than dust when I touched them. Twice I hit my head on something sharp under the house, and when I started ducking, then I hit my shoulder and back on it three more times, something up there tearing my shirt and cutting me, it felt like.

I beat on the floor again, just to say I had, I guess, that I'd tried everything I could, and I pushed back into the farthest corner of the skirt. My idea was that I could push my way out—from this side, the overlap would help me—make some kind of suicidal dash for the pump house roof, which I would magically fly up onto. Fear would give me wings, I don't know.

I didn't get all the way to the crack of light in the skirt, though.

Instead, I planted my hand into . . . a nest?

It was tacky and scratchy both at once, like whatever was living there had pulled all the broken things under the trailer under it, and then slobbered all over them until the trash went soft, could get shaped.

Only—not a nest, no. I looked with hands, traced out the contours.

A nest is open at the top.

This was more like a burst-open chrysalis.

One with a pocket deep down big enough for three of me.

My first thought was bobcats, since that was supposedly why the neighbor had all these dogs—bobcats had used to steal his grandfather's chickens, so now it was a forever war—except this didn't smell remotely feline. It didn't smell like anything, really. And animals always have a scent, don't they? Even the hunter animals, the reason they face into the wind, it's that they don't want their scent to get ahead of them, give them away.

Not this hunter.

It could come from any direction.

"Even the front door," I heard myself say.

Dad?

I didn't say it this time, didn't know if I wanted it to be real, didn't know if what started there could gestate or incubate or pupate into the kind of silhouette I'd felt crossing behind me in the living room. That I'd seen crossing the kitchen.

But you have to come from something, don't you?

I told myself yes, you had to.

Because—because a ghost, it's basically useless, it's just a vision, a phantasm. It doesn't even make sense that it could interact with light, much less a floor or a person or clothes. Meaning it had to have some kind of *organic* beginning, right?

I was still nodding, figuring this out.

When you come back from the dead, you're a spirit, you're nothing, just some leftover intention, some unassociated memory. But then, then what if a cat's sneaked into a dark space like this, right? What if that cat comes here to die, because it got slapped out on the road or hit by an owl or something, so it lays back in the corner to pant it out alone. Except, in that state, when it's hurt like that, when this cat isn't watching the way it usually does, something else can creep in. Something dead.

It's the injury that opens the door, I knew. The corruption.

But a cat isn't a person.

Now that cat that's not dying, is just panting, it has to wait for something else to crawl in, and then something else, and a third and fourth and finally some fiftieth thing. Just one worm at a time. You can build a self like that, if you compact it all together. If you remember how you used to be.

And if someone up in the living part of the house, if they remembered you too.

Dad was back because he loved us, yes. But it was also because I believed in him.

"*Dad!*" I said then, beating again on the floor of the house with the flat of my hands.

My face was muddy, I know, from the dust sifting

down onto my tears and snot.

There was more daylight where the dogs were digging now. Almost enough daylight.

I pushed back into the nest, into where Dad had been rebirthed, and my left hand felt out something more regular than the rest.

I brought it up, couldn't see it.

Three pushes over was the crack at the top of two panels. Just enough light.

I held my find up.

It was Dino's superhero action figure.

It was whole now, like it had never been bitten through.

I smiled, understood: this was what I'd been telling Mom. Exactly. Dad was here to fix Dino. To help him. I was holding the proof right here in my hands.

I stuffed it into my pocket.

It was all about timing, now.

Just—the problem was there were *four* dogs, not one. With one, I could wait until it slithered under the skirt, then push through on this side, race for the pump house. With four dogs, though, they'd have to one-at-a-time it. Meaning that if I pushed through right when one crawled under, that would give the three waiting their turn a chance to hear me, come barreling around the side of the house.

And if I waited until all four crawled under, then the

first would be to me by the time the fourth was crawling under, and I'd never get to push out.

There was no way to win.

I told my mom I was sorry. I told Dino his numbers up through twelve, and told him not to laugh about "8" like he always did. It could be funny, his funny snowman, but let it be secret-funny, and just keep going, on to nine and ten and eleven and twelve.

I told my dad it wasn't his fault. That he never would have left us. That that truck had probably been going to blow a rod any day now anyway.

I was crying hard by then. From fear, from feeling sorry for myself. I was even already picturing ahead to what Dino would find when he got home from the bus stop alone. The dogs probably would have dragged me out front. Would I even still be a body? Would he play with it like it was just a squirrel or a cat they'd torn into? And would he then have to grow up knowing that it had been my thigh meat he'd flipped over three times, to see how much dirt would stick to it?

Mom would know right off, of course.

I hoped she wouldn't blame herself for moving us here. I hoped all kinds of things, except what finally happened, right at the last moment, when there was a yellowy-white head under the skirt, snapping and snarling, in a frenzy.

What happened was footsteps crossed the floor of our house with authority. With impatience. Heavy footsteps.

And then the door opened, shut, and the first dog squealed.

Then the next, and the next, and then that yellowy-white head that was pushed under the skirt, it stayed there. But blood was coming from the mouth now.

My breath hitched twice—I was about to scream, I couldn't help it, it was welling up from a place deeper than I could tamp down—and I stood all at once, to just leave this place, this scene, this everything, and what I stood into was a strut or a pipe or I didn't know what, just that it was one thousand times more solid than me.

My face washed cold, my fingers tingled like they were going to sleep all at once, and all I knew with the world tunneling down from black to blacker, it was to claw for that one line of light I could see.

~

I woke with my mom hugging me to her. It was still daytime. She was holding me to her and she was screaming to someone, at someone.

It was the neighbor. He was on his knees with his hands behind his back. There was a shotgun on the ground before him, broken over. That's how I knew it was a shotgun.

When I could see around my mom better, there was a sheriff's deputy there. He was tall. His hat was on the ground. I kept looking from his hat to his head, like I didn't understand they could separate.

The sirens in the air were the ambulance, coming for the way my head was bleeding.

When the paramedics reached down for me, I shrunk away from their monstrous silhouettes, my breath going deep again, so my mom went with me. It was sixteen stitches. I didn't even feel them. The reason I didn't, it was that I think I finally went into shock, being led past our porch, where the dogs had been digging. Where the tetherball pole and wheel still were, the pole standing up now.

The whole front of our house was splashed with blood that had dried while I was knocked out.

And—this was the theory—evidently I'd sleepwalked again, once my conscious mind lost its grip.

Laid over the eyes of each destroyed dog were pieces of black fabric. Even the yellowy-white dog-head that had been left behind under the skirt, it had been pulled out, got the blinder treatment. On that dog the blindfold was more like a mask. Its tongue lolled out, was swelling.

The whole time I was getting stitched, the neighbor

was yelling that I was a menace, that I wasn't natural, that I wasn't right. That a human couldn't do this to four dogs, and any human that did needed to be put down, and that it was his God-given duty to do just that, he didn't care how many deputies the county sent.

Even when the sheriff's deputy guided him into the back of the cop car, the guy was still going off.

He'd come over with a gun, after his dogs. He wasn't coming home for a few days at least, my mom told me. And when he did, he'd be under strict orders from the sheriff himself, probably. She smoothed my hair down on the uncut side of my head and told me that if I even stubbed my toe in the future, that neighbor would probably go to jail.

Dino was just standing by Mom's leg, watching me.

I was now the brother who had taken on the dogs next door, and won.

Except it hadn't been me.

The sheriff's deputy kind of knew it too, I think. In his job, you see what a human body can and can't do, I imagine. You assess a scene right when you walk onto it, so you can apportion blame out appropriately. And some of it comes down to simple laws of nature.

Can a slight twelve-year-old tear into a pack of dogs like that, when each one of those dogs outweighs him?

Never mind that they said I was groggy when Mom

got there, called in by Dino, who couldn't count to twelve but was able to read her number off the wall well enough, dial it into the phone.

That was the real miracle of the day, as far as I was concerned.

Mom just pulled me to her again, when the ambulance and the sheriff's deputy were pulling away. When it was quiet at last.

Where I'd been when she found me, she said, it was halfway crawled through the house skirt over at the corner, under her bedroom. It wasn't a question, exactly. But I could have answered it, I think.

I didn't.

She didn't ask after her last black dish towel. The one I would have had to get inside the house to unfold from its drawer. I had a key, but why would I have relocked the door behind me? Why would I have come outside at all, with the dogs there? Why was I even *home* at all?

The way I would have torn the dish towel into even strips, though, I imagined I would have done that with my teeth, starting the tear at the edge, then pulling steady down in a straight line, three times. My hands bloody from not holding my own head, and not from hammering them into the ground with the wheel-base of the tetherball pole, but from grabbing the four dogs at both ends and, one by one, tearing them in two.

About dusk, the sheriff's deputy came back in his personal truck and shone his lights onto the front of our house, the light coming through our window bright enough, it threw Dino and my shadow onto the back wall by the television. We were standing in the window, watching him shovel up what was left of the dogs.

He lifted the remains into the back of the truck, and then the deputy stepped onto the porch and we shrunk back.

Mom talked to him at the door in muttery tones we couldn't get any words from, and they didn't hug at the end of it or anything. But I think they could have.

For Dad, I pretended not to see.

~

After stew from the can—mine and Dino's favorite, because stew came with unlimited club crackers we could lick the salt off first—Mom screwed a different lightbulb into the porch and dragged a rake back and forth across the dirt in front of the porch.

The reason she got a different lightbulb, it was that when she'd turned it on for the sheriff's deputy, it had shone red, had been misted or splashed or clumped with gore—I never saw the actual bulb, just the bloody light it smeared onto the porch. The sheriff's deputy had unscrewed it, tossed it into the back of his truck like nothing. Just more trash to be dumped at some dead-end pit out in the pasture.

He had taken the big parts, and now Mom was working the smaller bits into the dirt.

I guessed about anything might grow up from there, now.

When Mom came back in, I could tell she wanted to ask me a thousand and one questions, but instead we just watched a detective show where the detective had a cool car, and then she made sure to tuck us each into our beds tight, and kiss us into place like she used to.

I woke hours later, thought I was finally dreaming at last, because I couldn't feel myself standing. That meant I was floating, right? Wrong. It meant my feet were asleep again. I'd deadfooted it out of bed. And I had the distinct feeling in my throat that I'd just been saying something.

That left me two questions at once: what had I been saying, and who had I been saying it to?

I was alone in the kitchen, the refrigerator open behind me, cold on the back of my thighs.

"Thank you," I said to the darkness, to the night. Because it seemed like what I should be saying, for that afternoon. For the dogs.

Instead of going back to bed like usual, like makes sense if you don't have a blanket, I dodged the creaky parts of the floor across to the couch, and laid there with my head cocked up on the arm. There was a line of glare in the dead television screen from the lamp and I watched it, blinking as little possible, because as soon as that line of light broke, that was going to mean something had passed between me and it. And, if it came from the right, that meant Dad was done with fixing Dino. And if it came from the left, that meant he was just getting started.

What I wanted was to see him again, for real. Not just thinking about how he must have been at my age. Not just building him up in my mind from the stories Mom told. Not just seeing him through his sisters' words, where they only remembered the best parts. I wanted to see him as the dogs had, in full regalia and facepaint.

Hell yes, they'd squealed. Not that it mattered.

Death hadn't even been able to stop him. Four big dogs didn't stand much of a chance, had they?

When the interstate lights finally blotted out, it wasn't because I was drifting off, it was because a body was there.

Dino.

He was saying my name, looking for me.

All over his back and stomach were cusswords and pictures that Mom hadn't seen, because he'd fallen asleep in his school clothes, watching the detective-and-his-car show. He'd got hot in the night, though, peeled out of his shirt.

"Deener," I said without sitting up.

He looked over to the sound of my voice, his face blank, not expecting anything. I led him back to our bathroom and used a washcloth with warm water to rub off all the words that had got written on him on the bus. All the pictures that had been drawn onto him because I wasn't there to stop it from happening.

In my head I told my dad I was sorry. That I would be there next time, and all the times after that, too.

Up under Dino's ear on the left side, there was a hickey, even. Which no way could be from lips. I'd seen the kids at school doing them other ways. The best way was to get someone to Uncle-Sam their chin—to squeeze their chin-skin tight, into a prune, until somebody came down from the top, slammed that hand off, bruising the skin—but there was some way that was kind of like frogging an arm muscle. I hadn't seen it close up. As near as I could tell, you pinched somebody's skin between your first two knuckles, then spit down onto it and twisted hard.

That was the image I had to have, of Dino's bus ride home.

I guided him by the shoulders back into bed. I'd been able to get all the ink off, but not the hickey under his ear.

You can't rub a bruise off, no matter how hot the water is.

The hickey was big, had to have been a high schooler, to have hands like that.

And how many people had trailed their lines of spit down?

I hated them all. I hated them so much, it made my eyes hot.

I tucked Dino in, kissed him in place just like Mom—he was groggy by then, probably didn't know who I was, exactly—and when I was standing back up, my eyes dragged across the reflection in his window.

There was a man standing in the doorway of Dino's room.

There were feathers coming off him at all angles.

He was just a shape, a shadow in the glass, but I knew him.

I closed my eyes, let him leave.

~

Two mornings later, at the bus stop, Dino counted to nineteen all by himself. And then he fell right into a seizure, the worst one yet.

One of the girls who carried her books with a strap, not a bag, she ran back to flag Mom down.

It was the second time the ambulance had come out.

At three hundred dollars per trip.

The sheriff's deputy showed up too and just watched, but afterward he said something to the medic who was the driver, and that medic shut his metal clipboard in a way that Mom had to look away from to cry about.

When the sheriff's deputy came to talk to her, she picked Dino up and ran inside, pulling me behind her.

I didn't know what was happening.

The sheriff's deputy sat out there for a while—I watched him from my bedroom window—and then he backed up, eased away, his left arm patting the outside of the door of his truck in a way that kind of made me know him.

Because Mom couldn't miss any more shifts—she also wasn't supposed to be late even one more time, but it was a little late for that, she said—I got to stay home from school with Dino. She explained to me that when your brother's sick, then you can count as sick too.

We weren't sick, though.

After she was gone, I used some kite string and a football to rig us some tetherball action, to make up for what had happened on the bus.

We batted the football back and forth, but the point hurt when it caught you in the head or the side, so we ended up playing a game where we would throw the ball like a football, like it probably wanted to be thrown. Who won was who got it to go around the most times before it touched the pole. I was the one who had to count the revolutions, but I did it out loud so Dino could chime in, help me complete the word of each number.

What I found was that if you threw downwards, sort of, you could get more times around. I explained it to Dino until he got it, had the idea he was going to have friends over at some point and would need to know how to win one game.

When he picked it up, that you throw down to make it go longer, I let him beat me three times with the trick. In between throws, I found myself always watching the dark cracks between the house skirts. It was funny: from inside, they were cracks of light, but out here, they were cracks of darkness.

I imagined Dad watching us from that crack.

His boys, his sons.

We were going to make it, I told him.

We were all right.

That night, after cornbread with beans cooked into it like Grandma used to make, I got my science notebook out. The one with the map I'd drawn of the interior of our house. I turned the page, made a chart now. It was Dino's seizures on the vertical arm. The only thing I could think to put on the horizontal arm, it was the idiots at the bus stop.

Was there a correlation? Was this a nerves thing to him? Did pressure or getting pushed around activate something in him that was already going wrong?

I drilled inky dots into the corner of the page, trying to think it all through, and finally decided I needed more data.

I was just getting started on the next page—on the scary silhouette of a fancydancer I was going to tell Mom was just anybody, just something I was making up—when Dino was standing in my doorway.

"The show," he said.

I sighed my best big-brother sigh, made a production of setting my notebook aside, and pulled my way across the room, down to the living room.

His show, he was right: there was a fuzz of static over it now.

"Tell me when it's better," I said to him, and went out the back door, sat down on the ground to twist the base of the tall antenna, try to find the signal, the door open behind me so Dino could call out when I found the sweet spot.

Mom came out and sat on the back steps and smoked a cigarette, watched the horizon, and, I think, me.

"You were talking about your father," she said.

"*Better yet?*" I called out to Dino, because I'd nearly worked the antenna all the way around in its base, and the wire was going to wrap soon.

"He's playing with his heroes," Mom said, shrugging like what could you do.

I gave up on the antenna.

"It's only natural," Mom said then, narrowing her eyes at a pair of headlights out on the interstate, maybe. Or just to get her words in order. "You're—the age you are, this is when you start really needing to have a dad around."

I pried a clod of dirt up, lobbed it at the propane tank just to watch it explode against all that silver paint.

"I'm all right," I told her.

This is the lie, when you're twelve. And all the other years, too.

You never tell your mom anything that might worry her. Moms have enough to worry about already.

"You do need a man around," she said anyway, then smushed her cigarette out on the second step from the top and deposited the butt in the coffee can she kept under the stairs, like hiding it.

Minutes after she'd gone back inside to get Dino started in his bed process, it hit me, what she was saying—no, what she was asking: What if that sheriff's deputy came over for dinner one night? Or to drag a harrows across all the packed dirt, so maybe something could grow up from it?

I lobbed another dirt clod at the propane tank, missed altogether, and then came down to my knees fast, scrabbling all the dirt clods and rocks to me that I could, to sling right into the heart of that propane tank.

Hit, hit, miss, hit.

I was breathing hard.

The skirt of the house, it was right behind me.

I turned, regarded it up and down its whole fourteen inches of long triangular darkness, and finally, like a trade, picked all Mom's old butts from the coffee can and pushed them through one at a time. It was an offering.

Then I put the can back but tipped it over like the wind might have blown it over, so it could get a last drag on all those cigarettes.

In my head I was walking the floor plan in my science notebook. I was a stick figure pacing the halls, looking in every room. On patrol.

The television wasn't working, you say?

Could it be because there was somebody under the floor right exactly there? Not because he wanted to hear that show better but because his youngest son was sitting right in front of that screen.

Indians, we don't have guardian angels—if we did, they'd have been whispering to us pretty hard when some certain ships bobbed up on the horizon—but we do have helpers. I think usually it's supposed to be an animal.

Maybe when you need more, though, maybe then you get a person.

Maybe then your father gets special permission to come back, so long as he stays hidden.

So long as nobody tries to rat him out.

Meaning, yes, it was me who'd killed those four dogs. It was me who laid that torn-in-four black dishcloth over their eyes.

And it was my fault the cartoon wouldn't play without static.

Just for luck, I dug up one more dirt clod, a big flat one, and aimed hard, slung it as hard as I could into the side of the propane tank.

It exploded exactly as I'd wanted it to: a big dusty cloud, billowing out and thinning.

Then that plume took on a dim glow.

I stepped one step up the back stairs, my hand to the knob of the door, and then I saw the glow for what it was.

The neighbor's back porch light.

He was home from jail.

~

Instead of asking the deputy sheriff over for dinner right

away, like all the cop shows said would happen, the deputy sheriff drove me and Dino to school the next three days. He'd heard what happened at the bus stop.

I just stared out the window on my side. I was playing the prisoner. I was being transported to my next holding facility. An armed guard was transporting me. He was under orders not to talk to me. Not that I was going to try.

On the way back from school, in the big empty space before you got to our clump of houses, he let Dino flip the switch that fired the sirens up. Later, while Mom was warming spaghetti and then forgetting she was warming spaghetti, I told Dino to shut up so I could hear the television. He was playing with his trucks in front of the couch and making siren sounds with his mouth.

Dino did stop, and then I had to watch the show I hadn't even been watching.

I just picked at my burned spaghetti.

That night when I was standing at the window, I was in my pants, not just my underwear. I was watching for the deputy sheriff's truck, now. To do what? I had no idea. Just to prove it to myself, I guess.

I tried not to blame Mom. She didn't know Dad was back, and she wouldn't believe me if I told her, and if I told her, it would make him leave, anyway. So, all I could do was watch.

I fell asleep with my head leaning against the glass and

the wall, and when I woke, I jerked around, to try to see a shape just stepping past.

The living room was empty.

But you're supposed to be getting more *solid,* I said inside.

Not more invisible.

Nothing invisible could have done that to the four dogs.

And—and Dino. He hadn't had a seizure for days now.

I pushed away from the window to go to bed, because nothing was working, because everything was stupid, and I nearly had my eyes pulled all the way away when I saw motion out front.

I'd thought the wheel at the base of the tetherball pole was going to be a truck with a thrown rod.

What I saw now told me maybe it was—that maybe the truck hadn't been dragged down here, but parts of it had come down all the same.

The wheel, maybe.

The football was going around the tall pole.

I smiled.

Because the front door squeaked and squealed—Mom said it was the best alarm—I went out the back door, by Dino's room. He could sleep through anything.

The football was just tapping into the pole by the time I came around the side of the house, having to test each step for sharpness before giving it my weight.

I let the football hang there for a few breaths, and then I picked it up, handed it around and around the pole until I had to walk it around.

It was my turn.

"Watch this," I said, and flung the ball at a spot in the dirt maybe six feet in front of me. The string grabbed it in a perfect parabola, flung it high and around, so I had to fall away from getting hit. I kept on falling, too, caught myself on my elbows.

That was why the headlights didn't spear me in place.

I stayed down, turned over onto my stomach.

The truck was just coasting, not turned on.

When the headlights turned to wash across the front of our house, they cut off just in time. Just the brake lights flaring in the barely there dust the tires had coughed up.

The sheriff's deputy.

Mom stepped out onto the porch, didn't turn the light on.

The sheriff's deputy guided his door shut, just one click deep, and followed her back inside.

I told my dad not to look, not to listen.

No lights glowed on in the house.

I rolled onto my back, stared straight up.

The football just hung there on its string.

I understood. Lying there then, I patted my pocket for the superhero I was just remembering, from the day all the dogs died. It wasn't there, had been too long, and these were the wrong pants anyway.

What I'd wanted to do, it was hold it up against the backdrop of all the stars so its silhouette could fly back and forth.

Except I wasn't a kid anymore.

I was the man of the house, at least until Dad got solid enough for Mom and Dino to see him too.

I stood, my hands balled into fists by my thighs.

I walked back to the house, my line taking me to the front door so I could open it, let it squeak and squeal, but then I stopped at the sheriff's deputy's truck.

The driver's side door opened easy, with no sound at all.

I sat there behind the wheel, my hand cupped over the dome light.

There was the siren switch right there.

I smiled, was slow-motion reaching for it and all the excitement it would bring to this night when I remembered how the sheriff's deputy had guided Dino's hand *there,* instead of to the glove compartment Dino had been going for, because, in our car, that's where Mom let him keep his road toys.

After checking the front door and all the windows again—nothing—I opened that glove compartment myself.

Tucked way back there was a short little revolver.

I held it in wonder, careful of where the barrel pointed, and then I looked to the front door again. And then I went in through the back of the house, testing each step again, because I was one pistol heavier now, plus however many shells it held.

~

This time I didn't have to be asleep, or just waking from it, to see Dad.

I'd had the pistol held low, pointed at the ground, and had only looked in Dino's room to be sure he was there, and not shaking under the covers.

What I saw nearly made me pull the trigger, shoot my foot off.

Dad—my years-dead father—he was leaned over Dino, had maybe been listening to his heart or whispering into his mouth. His fingertips were to either side of Dino's sleeping shape, and he had one knee on the bed, one foot on the ground. And he was looking across the room like an animal, right into my soul. His eyes shone, not with light but with a kind of wet darkness. The mouth too—no, the lips. And curling up from them was smoke. From the cigarettes and ashes I'd funneled behind the skirt.

My breath choked in my throat thinking about that,

that taste, and I wavered in place there in the hall, caught between a scream and a fall, and when I sensed a body behind me, in the back door that was just a doorway because I'd left it open, I knew it was because I'd looked away from Dad in Dino's bedroom. That I'd broken eye contact just long enough for him to step around the rules of the physical world come out here with me for a little father-son discussion.

And—just because he couldn't get whatever he needed from my neck, that didn't mean he didn't still have hands.

The big pistol jerked up almost on its own, my arm straight behind it, and my finger was already pulling the trigger over and over into the middle of that darkness, that body.

What I was saying inside, if anything, it was to stay away from my little brother. That you're not helping anymore. That I'm sorry, I'm sorry, but—the shots cracked the world in half, then quarters, then slivers of itself.

The flashes from the end of the barrel were starbursts of orange shot through with black streaks, and they strobed the inside of the hall bright white. And my shots, because of the recoil, because of the way the barrel jumped up each time I pulled the trigger, they were climbing from the midsection, higher and higher.

Five.

I shot five times.

And the sound—I heard the first one deep in my head, and felt the other four in my shoulder, in my jaw, in the base of my spine.

I know it's too fast for tears to have come, but the way I remember it, I was crying and screaming while I shot.

It was the worst thing ever.

It was my dad.

I was killing him again, wasn't I?

He'd clawed and fought his way back to us, and he'd come back better, he'd come back in the regalia he'd been supposed to wear, before everything else found him.

And he danced. He was dancing now, with each shot.

First his right side flung out, his arm following, and then his left, from the next bullet, and then, for just an instant, there was a clean hole right through the middle of the front of his head. Through his face.

Just ten minutes ago, we'd been playing catch with the football.

When you grow up with a dead father, this isn't something you ever expect to get to do. It had felt like cheating. It had been the best thing ever.

But now it was over.

Because—I had to say it, just to myself—because he'd been feeding on Dino, I was pretty sure.

The wet lips. The empty eyes.

Dino's seizures had started before I'd seen Dad walking across the living room, but that didn't mean he hadn't been making that trip for three or four weeks already, then, did it?

Dino was never going to set any math records, but his counting, it had been going all right, anyway. He was last in his class, was on special watch, was a grade or two behind. But whatever Dad was drinking from him, whatever Dad needed from him in order to get whole again, to come back, it was something Dino needed.

It made me hate him.

That fifth time I pulled the trigger, the last shot?

It was the most on-purpose of any of them.

I was holding that revolver with both hands by then, a stance I knew from TV. I was trying to get the front of the barrel to stop hopping up.

The fifth shot, it went center mass. That was a term I knew from the cop shows, too.

Dino, he knew all about dinosaurs and fairies and talking cars, from what he watched.

Me, I knew about justice.

And, thinking back on it now, we're lucky not to have all blown up that night, from one of my shots hitting the propane tank.

I was shooting at someone taller than me, though. That was the thing. It meant my shots were more or less pointing upwards, and climbing, once they splashed through.

All that was behind us was empty pasture.

One with a few more ounces of lead in it now. A few shards sprinkled down, coated in blood for the bugs to crawl over and lick, if bugs even have tongues.

All this in maybe three seconds.

A lifetime, sure. But an instant, too.

The world was so quiet, after all that sound. And because I was deaf.

I let the pistol thunk to the floor.

It hit on the barrel, tumped over into my bare ankle. I flinched away, took a step forward to see what I'd done.

Lying on his back just past the back stairs was the neighbor, who'd come for me just like he'd said he was going to. A different shotgun was clamped in his hands like if he just held on to it, he couldn't fall back through whatever he was falling through, because its length would snag, would hold him up.

It didn't.

He had no face, had a mass of bubbling red for a body.

My chest sucked in, my whole body kind of undulating, and when I looked up, it was because the sheriff's deputy was standing beside me, naked.

A lot of grown men would have simply backhanded the upstart twelve-year-old punk who had taken a gun, unloaded it out the back door like that, just for attention.

Not this sheriff's deputy.

His name was Larsen.

Years later he would run for sheriff.

His campaign speech probably didn't include driving his knee into my side, so that I ragdolled over into the paneled wall. He probably didn't put on any of his posters the way he didn't let me fall but held me up with his left hand, for his right fist to drive into my teeth.

I was a murderer, though.

Killers, they deserve what they get, don't they? You cash in your rights when you start blowing people away like I just had.

By the sheriff's deputy's third punch, my mom was riding his arm.

Me, I was on the carpet by then, my head turned to Dino's open doorway.

He was standing in it, his face slack, a thin line of clear water seeping down from behind his ear.

I took a picture of him in my head to save for later—for all the jail and cameras and whatever was coming.

It's a picture I've still got.

~

None of us left the house the next day. Not me or Dino for school—it's not like we had grades to wreck, really—and not Mom, for work. It would mean she'd have to get another job, probably something at night instead of day, but that was all for later.

We sat on the couch and watched whatever the television gave us.

There was so much static we could hardly tell who was who.

When Mom finally turned it off with the bulky old controller, the curvy green screen reflected the three of us back at ourselves.

The sheriff's deputy—I didn't bother knowing his name until high school—wasn't there.

Mom hadn't just scratched him. She'd grown up on the reservation, I mean. She'd started fighting on the playground, had moved on to parking-lot scraps, and had even crashed a vase into someone's face at a wake once. When the sheriff's deputy had finally left, he'd left limping, and had to crank the window on his door down with the wrong hand.

And no more deputies showed up. Not the sheriff either.

I stared at my shape in the television screen, sure that next time we turned it on, that outline would stay but it would get filled in with my face. NATIVE AMERICAN

ALMOST-TEEN SHOOTS NEIGHBOR OVER PETS, or some-thing like that.

But. Except.

Where was everybody?

Why was I still here?

Did it have to do with the fact that I'd used the sheriff's deputy's drop-piece—I knew the term—and not his department-issued service revolver? Would turning me in mean he was turning himself in?

It didn't track.

For most of the night I'd been in a daze, Mom trying to get my lips and nose and ear to stop bleeding. It wasn't shock, but it wasn't being completely awake, either.

Now I was awake. All the way awake, my heart pounding.

When the sheriff's deputy had left, he'd left alone.

He'd left once before with the dead—evidence—shoveled into the back of his truck.

This time he'd just left it for us to deal with.

For me to deal with.

I wormed away from Mom and the blanket, guided Dino's arm onto her leg instead of mine, and went to the sink first, for the coffee cup of water I didn't want. But I needed an excuse to untangle from the living room.

Next was the bathroom I didn't need, at the end of the hall.

On the way there, I stopped to whisper the back door open.

There was no body. No blood.

I swallowed a lump, stepped out to be sure. Then down the three wooden steps, the soles of my feet ready for the splinters I knew I deserved.

Maybe ten feet to my right, one section of the skirt was ... it wasn't *flapping* shut, exactly. This was slower. This was that piece of corrugated tin or aluminum or whatever being *held*, and guided back to its careful overlap.

I was breathing too deep now. I missed a step, my foot going through to the coffee can ashtray, the lip of the can scraping the back of my ankle, the sole of my foot whumping into the ash, sighing that smoky smell up into the air all around me.

But I could still see. I had to see.

There were drag marks in the dirt.

Not from just now, but from—I guessed from when I was getting punched into the carpet in the hall. When I was staring into Dino's room.

Dad.

If a cat and bugs and drinks from Dino could bring him far enough back to drag a full-grown, shot-dead man under the house, then what could a full-grown, shot-dead corpse do for him?

I pulled back inside the house, shut the door, twisted

the dead bolt, and hated that I had to call it that in my head.

~

After the weekend, which mostly involved me standing in Dino's doorway all night, then falling asleep on the couch to cartoons, we were at the bus stop again. The sixth-graders and even the seventh-graders either gave us room, or they didn't see what worse they could do to my face that wasn't already done. Mom said that if the school tried to call Child Services on her, to tell them to call the sheriff's department, too.

Walking past the neighbor's chainlink, there'd been no dogs to harass us. And no neighbor to harass us, either.

How long until he was missed? Was he on probation now? Was he going to skip a check-in soon, and then the next check-in as well?

I hadn't been under the house again.

There had to be a matted nest of hair and grass and saliva pulsating down there, though. Not pushed into the corner anymore but probably dug into the ground, in case I pulled all the skirts off at once, let the light in. I wasn't sure whether what I was seeing in the secret parts of my head were my dad trying to crawl inside a corpse, wear it like more regalia, or if he was drinking it in somehow. All I *did* know was that if I uncovered him down there, then there would be a corpse riddled with bullet holes under our house, and that corpse would belong to a neighbor we already had bad history with.

Everything was screwed.

Soon Dad was going to be solid enough, he could just knock on the door. Except he wouldn't knock, I knew.

I always thought—I think anybody would think this—that when you come back from the dead like he had, that you're either out to get whoever made you dead, or you're there because you miss your people, are there to help them somehow.

The way it was turning out, it was that you could maybe come back, be what you'd always meant to be, but to do that, you had to latch on to your people and drink them dry, leave them husks. After that, you could walk off into your new life, your second chance. With no family to hold you back.

It wasn't fair.

He was going to be out there on the pow-wow circuit, taking every purse, walking out into the campers and lodges and back seats with whatever new girl, and nobody would ever know what he'd had to do to us in order to dance like that. After a few years, he'd probably even stay on one of those other reservations, have two more sons. Ones who weren't broken. Ones he could teach things to, ones he could tell stories to.

It made me want to throw our tethered football so hard into the ground that the whole pole fell down.

Game over.

School was school, like always.

Teachers reading to us from lesson plans, hands going up, trays of food getting doled out. In the bathroom, with a dollar I'd stolen from my mom's purse, I bought a tube of cinnamon toothpicks. They were the hot thing at this school—everybody trying to outburn the last batch. I threaded one between my teeth, but the liquid cinnamon the tube was swimming with found the cuts in my lip and gums, and made my eyes water.

"Perfect," the guy who'd sold me it said, and patted me on the shoulder, left me there by the paper-towel dispenser.

After school, I made Dino watch cop shows with me. Which meant he did what he always did: melted off the couch like I wouldn't notice, dug his toys out from under the coffee table, and walked and flew and drove them across the carpet between me and the television.

The way I knew Dad could smell him, that he was right under that part of the floor now, it was that the show went all static.

He was up, then. Out of the ground, cracked out of his chrysalis, however it worked. It didn't even matter anymore. Figuring it all out wouldn't change how any of it had to go.

What could we do against him?

Nothing.

Even if he wasn't dead or a ghost, he would still be our dad, wouldn't he? What could a sixth-grader and a third-grader and a mom do against a dad? When they're drinking, you can slip away, hide. But the only thing Dad was going to be drunk on, it was us.

Dino, at least.

Was that I was supposed to do, to save me and Mom? Leave Dino like an offering? Trade him for both of us?

None of the cops on my shows would ever do that. Even for the worst criminal.

Because of justice. Because of what's right.

Dino flew a superhero action figure up into the air to swoop back down against some convoy of dinosaurs—dinosaurs on the trailers of trucks, all lined up—and I recognized it as the one I'd rescued from under the house. Meaning I'd left it in my pocket, Mom had found it in the laundry, and she'd returned it back to Dino's room. It's the natural life cycle of toys. Even ones that had been bitten through, partially digested, then somehow been born again, whole.

The reason I could see that superhero action figure so crisp, it was all the snow behind it on screen.

When it swooped down, though, the cop show cleared up.

Instead of telling Dino to do that again—fat chance—I waited for it to happen on its own.

A T. rex batted the superhero back, and he tumbled up into the crackly white snow background then gathered himself, angled himself down, leading with his left fist, and when he came at that open-mouthed, ready-for-battle heavy metal T. rex, my detective on-screen cuffed another perp. The picture was clear enough I could see the tiny key he was holding between his teeth, that he spit down into the drain in the curb just to show this bad guy how soon he was getting out of these particular handcuffs.

I didn't care about the show anymore, though.

That night, after Mom had lingered too long in each of our rooms like she wanted to say she was sorry—for what?—and after she'd stopped with the dishes in the kitchen, I crept into Dino's room with my sloshing tube of toothpicks. What gave them their extra kick, I'd heard, it was a single drop of mace stolen from a mother's purse.

"Turn your head," I said down to Dino, and he did it without questioning, in a way that made me hate myself, and the whole world.

The hickey hidden behind his ear, I should have known it for a spigot the moment I saw it. You couldn't grab any skin there, where it's pulled so tight to the bone. Where there's no meat, no muscle.

Was that what made it good for Dad? Was he drawing something from the inside of Dino's bones? Would Dino's kneecaps also be raw in the same way? The knobby parts of his wrist?

He wasn't getting clumsy, though.

He was getting slow. Numbers were slipping out of his head. Into my dead father's mouth.

The hickey was worse now too. Deeper, darker, rougher in a way that made me think of a cat's tongue.

I uncorked the tube, wet my index finger, and painted that red with heat.

Dino tensed up, every muscle in his little body tensing, but he didn't turn his head around.

This wasn't new to him.

"It's to make you better," I whispered to him.

His eyes were squinched shut. He nodded yes, okay, do it, but I was done already.

I nudged him with the back of my fingers.

He looked up to me and breathed out, clear drool stringing down into his pillow in a way that made me think of lake water. The kind people drown in.

Standing there, I promised myself that if I ever had kids, I was going to be different.

It's a promise every Indian kid makes at some point.

You mean it when you say it, though. You mean it so hard.

~

The second time I saw my dead father cross from the kitchen doorway to the hall that led back to the utility room, and to my little brother's room, it was technically my thirteenth birthday. With everything that had happened that week, the only one who remembered was my PE teacher. It was because we'd all had to put our birth dates on a fitness form, and he'd ordered them on the wall by those dates for some reason known only to PE teachers.

Without him telling me, I might have forgotten too.

My feet were cold, the beds of my toenails blue.

This time I'd used shoelaces to crimp the circulation off. Because they make better knots. And I'd done each leg by itself so I wouldn't fall over first thing.

I couldn't fake sleep, and couldn't risk it since there was no trigger for sleepwalking that I knew, but I *was* tired from standing guard the last few nights. And from my face trying to knit itself back into some semblance of myself. I'd nodded off a time or two, I mean. At least I know I'd woken with my top lip dried to the window glass—the reason it was my top lip was that when a face eases forward to a window, and when the neck muscles abandon it in sleep, it slides down until the top lip rolls back to wet, stops that slow fall.

When I licked my tongue back into my mouth, it tasted like metal. It didn't make sense, but maybe glass doesn't have its own taste. Maybe that's why drinks come in it.

What I wanted to do, it was dream. Or, no, I wanted more. I wanted to dream and to remember it.

The next time I woke, it was because something had woke me, I knew.

It's a different kind of waking up when there's still the ghost of a sound in the small bones of your ear.

It was the floor in the living room, creaking.

It meant Dad was solid now. That he had weight to give, and be careful of.

Maybe he was just now realizing it too.

At least, there hadn't been a second creak yet.

I could see his reflection in the glass, dim and close.

Full regalia. The fancydancer he'd always meant to be.

My dad.

My throat was shaking. My heart would be his drumbeat.

"When you died," I told him, like I'd been saving up since I was four, "I was all crying. You probably know. But it wasn't for you. I was crying because Mom was crying.

I was crying because of your sisters. I couldn't even remember what you looked like, until the wake."

No response.

But—I was listening with every part of my body—there was a breath, finally.

He was learning that again too, then.

"And Deener, he doesn't even remember you at all," I said.

My plan was for this to core him out somehow. But my plan, it hinged on him still caring about us.

Really, he only needed us to convert into a future he'd already assumed was going to be real.

Not if I could help it.

I turned around all at once, the superhero action figure held tight in my fist like a weapon—I had no idea what it could do to him, just that it was connected, that because part of it had passed through Dino, it mattered, was some sort of tether—but he was gone, had kept on walking. Maybe seconds and seconds ago.

If he was solid enough to creak, to breathe, then maybe this was the last night, then. Maybe this was the night he drank Dino dry, left him open-eyed and dead in his bed, another tragedy at the poverty line.

And because Dino had already been slowing down, or, really, topping out, he was the only one Dad could take from, finally. It made Dino have something inside him that I didn't have, that Mom didn't have.

Still, Dino having to die like that, us trying to deal with it, to keep living—it wouldn't happen.

Mom would collapse into herself a hundred times a day, wouldn't be able to work any shifts for a year, for two, and I would walk down to the bus stop with a two-by-four, and I wouldn't stop until there was nothing left of any of them down there. And then the sheriff's deputy would come for me like he'd always known he'd have to someday, and Mom would take off with me in the Buick, just driving straight across the pasture, for the mountains, for the memory of mountains, both her hands on the steering wheel, and this is already the way Indians have been dying for forever.

And it would be Dad killing us.

I shook my head no against all of that and ran for the hall, made it just in time to see Dad come reeling out of Dino's room, his mouth open wide, so I could see that it wasn't teeth in there at all but wrinkly black muscle, like a worm.

What he was recoiling from, what he was trying to brush away from his mouth, it was the heat I'd left there. The cinnamon, the mace.

In order to make a connection as deep as he was making with Dino, he had to touch the most raw part of himself to that tight skin behind Dino's ear.

I hadn't even planned on him getting that far, though.

We were supposed to still be having a big standoff in the living room.

What was supposed to happen, it was me striding right past him into the kitchen, and dunking that superhero into the dishwater Mom had left for the pans to soak in.

He'd drowned once, my father. I was going to drown him again.

He was going to stand there in the living room and spit up white, bubbly water, and he was going to fall to his knees, reach out for me to stop. But I wouldn't.

I didn't even have a real plan for what to do with his body, with the corpse that was not going to make any sense at all to Mom, but first was killing him. After that, I would figure the rest out.

Only, now, he was banging back in the hall. Into the back door.

It flapped open and he held on to both sides for a moment, long enough for me to see that his eyes weren't shiny black anymore. The pupils or irises or whatever were still too big, bigger than human, what you'd probably need for living in the dead space under a house, but there was some white at the edges now too.

It was how I could tell he was looking at me.

It was how I could see everything he wanted to do to me.

I ran ahead, my arms already straightened, and pushed him the rest of the way out, then stood there, my chest heaving.

He didn't fall up into the sky. There wasn't any rule about that, evidently. He could be outside or he could be inside.

Because he was solid now, though, that meant gravity could pull on him.

He'd fallen backwards down the steps, had landed hard on the packed dirt. Meaning there was still time for me to rush and fall back to the kitchen, dunk the super-hero in the dishwater and hold it there. But, it would take two, three minutes to work, wouldn't it?

Those would be two or three minutes I wouldn't have a line of sight on him. Two or three minutes he could have with Dino.

It might be all he needed.

I slammed the superhero into the weather-strip edge of the doorframe face first, but nothing happened.

No choice, then. The kitchen. I had to try.

When Dad took his first step toward me, I was already falling back, one hand to the paneling in the hall, to guide me to the glow of the range light Mom always left on, the only part of the stove that always worked when you hit the button.

I swayed my back away from the thick fingertips reaching

for me, and it threw me enough off balance that I slipped on the linoleum of the kitchen, hit a chair, sent it tumbling into the living room, my right hand already clawing for the handle of the refrigerator door. I caught it as barely as I'd ever caught anything, but then the door opened and I slung out farther with it, Dad's knee or shoulder or head slamming the door, stopping it dead in its arc.

It shut back hard, taking its light with it, and the fingerprints of my middle and ring finger, it felt like, and then Dad was standing there, his regalia making him so much taller than the refrigerator, the darkness making him still a silhouette.

I'd fallen with my back to the cabinet, a sharp metal handle digging into my shoulder.

"Not—not Deener," I said, and pushed one hand up behind me, like to use that hand to pull myself up.

But what that hand was holding was the superhero action figure.

It slipped into the cold water, and then—

~

—and then the water, it was lapping all around us. Around both of us.

It was night. Outside. And the air was crisper somehow. No: thinner.

We were on the reservation.

It was trees all around, except under us right now. Under us right now, there was water.

We were in the shallows of the lake, and—and I was taller, I was grown. I couldn't see my face, but my hands, my arms, my boots, I didn't know them. I'd never known them.

And then it hit me: the same way that, when sleepwalking, I was kind of inhabiting *myself*, that's what I was doing here. Just, now I was inhabiting someone *else*. Someone before. Someone who had sneaked up on a dying campfire by walking around the whole edge of the lake, numbing his feet, leaving him open for me to inhabit. Someone who had been looking for my dad ever since my dad had left a certain truck in the ditch, a rod thrown through the block.

I had access to this truck owner's memories, too, and remembered them like they'd *happened* to me: two days ago, Dad—"Park" in this memory—had come over because he knew where a moose was. He'd seen it twice over the last week. *Twice.*

This wasn't some big dumb cow, either, my dad had said. *Park* had said. This was a proper bull.

Forget the meat. That kind of rack, Park knew a guy down in the city who would go fifteen hundred for it, in velvet like that. He already had the rifle borrowed, and already had a chainsaw himself. All he needed now was a truck, so he could stake out that curve by the little pond, then pop them a high-dollar moose, saw the head off, carry it direct to that guy he knew, the rack wrapped in plastic bags so all the velvet wouldn't dry up, blow away before he could get there.

Fifteen hundred, split two ways.

And he'd said he'd return the truck with a full tank of gas, even.

It was easy money. The easiest money.

Just like that, even though I knew better, I'd worked the square-headed key off my ring, passed it across, and didn't see the truck again until four days later. Until yesterday.

It had been on the side of the road, abandoned, walked away from.

There wasn't an actual rod thrown through the hood, but I'd figured that part out soon enough.

I hadn't gone back to work that afternoon, or all day today.

Park had been hunting a moose. Now I was hunting Park.

Where I found him was sitting by a dying fire, beer cans lined in a circle all around it. Just, on the way to finding him, he became Dad. Not because he'd changed. Because I had.

I stood there in the water, watching him like a spirit come up from the deep.

When he looked up, he even said my name: "Junior." Then he said it three more times, softer and softer: "Junior Junior Junior."

Every fourth person on our reservation, that's their name, like the same stupid person is trying life after life until he gets it right at last.

Still, *this* Junior was me, now, not the one he'd loaned the truck to. Maybe it was because we had the same name that I was able to go back, inhabit him, *be* him, or maybe that action figure, this was his heroic power—to grant the one thing that can save a little brother.

Dad offered me his beer and I swatted it away, liked this new strength, this new, adult reach.

Right now, the four-year-old me was twenty miles south, dying from pneumonia—maybe from how cold it was where this me was standing right now.

There are rules, I know.

Not knowing them doesn't mean they don't apply to you.

I couldn't stop looking at him either, my dad. Not just from this other Junior's height, but at *all*.

This was the Dad that Mom had known. That she had loved. That she had thought was going to last forever.

He was still young. Stupid too, you could tell just from

the way his eyes were, you could tell from his loopy grin, but he would get better. He would figure this all out. He would come home, wouldn't he? All his sisters told my mom he would. She just had to wait.

"It wasn't there, man," he said, shrugging.

"The moose or the truck?" I must have said, since I heard myself saying it, even though it wasn't my voice.

"Third gear," my dad said back, snuffling a laugh out, and like that, I had crossed to him right through the dead fire, was kneeing him in the face. He rolled backwards out of his trashed-out lawn chair and I went with him, my arm a piston, my fist the hammer at the end of it.

Dad, though, he wasn't even fighting back. That was the thing. He just kept holding his hands out to the side, saying this was okay, he deserved this, do my worst. It was like—it was like he knew who was inside this Junior. Like he couldn't fight back, since it was his son. Like he knew he deserved this for what he hadn't even done yet. Like he knew I'd dove into a sink miles and years away, come up in the shallows of this lake.

I don't know what he thought, finally. I don't know what he knew.

Just that I had to save Dino. No matter how much it hurt.

I pushed Dad back as hard as I could, and he sat down in the shallows of the lake, was still kind of laughing.

"What are you . . . What are we *doing*, Junior, man?" he said, shaking the wet from his fingertips, his mouth running blood down onto his chest.

I stood there in front of him, the cold water lapping over my feet, and knew this could end now. That it *should* end here. It was just a truck.

But—maybe this is the way it had always been, every time this happened.

For the truck, Junior was just going to deal out a beating, a shaming.

To keep Dino safe, I was going to have to wade farther out.

That's why nobody ever got sent up for it. This is why Junior never told anybody about this—even whoever his girlfriend had been eight years ago.

Because he didn't know about it.

He didn't know the why of it.

He was sleepwalking.

There were just two people here in the shallows. Not three. Me and Dad. Me finally getting to see him as he was, as I'd always wanted to see him, as I'd always dreamed of seeing him. And then having to step forward, knee him hard enough in the face that a line of blood slings up behind and above him.

He falls into the water, and the blood goes out farther.

And then I'm on him, my knee to his chest, my hands

to his face, to push it back, to push it under the surface.

It's for leaving us. It's for coming back.

I'm screaming right into the top of the water, and his eyes are open inches away, his hair floating all around, and then, right at the end, he opens his mouth, breathes in what he can't.

I hold him there for longer, to be sure. And then for longer after that, hugging him to me, which is probably a blurry image the other Junior still remembers in jagged bits. And then I push him out like a raft, and I slam my hand into the top of the water over and over, the splashing droplets stinging my face harder each time, but never hard enough.

What floats in around me, from behind me, are porcupine quills, and feathers, and plastic beads.

I stand away from all that, and when I look back—

~

—it's to an empty kitchen, miles and years away from then.

But there's water on the floor where Dad was standing.

I edge closer to it, then rush past it, sure that where he's retreated, it's to Dino's room, because he can fix all this, because it's not too late.

Where he is, it's through the back door, the wooden

steps wet with his staggering footprints. Where he is, it's facedown against the packed dirt, his hand reaching ahead of him.

This is what it's like to kill your father.

This is what it's like to kill everything your father could have been, if only the world hadn't found him, done its thing to him.

"Don't come back again," I said down to him, my throat filling with tears like I was drowning too, and then Dino was standing beside me in his nightshirt, his expression emptier than it should have been. Even if he didn't recognize Dad, still, there was a dead man in full fancydance regalia lying dead in the dirt four feet from us.

It was all the same to Dino.

"One, two, three, four," he said, one side of his mouth smiling.

He said it again—"*Four*"—and I tracked where he was wanting me to look.

Standing just past where Dad was dead, there were the shapes of four dogs.

The yellowy-white one padded forward, pushed its nose into Dad's neck, and I breathed in fast, let go of Dino's hand so I could put my palm to his chest, to keep him from trying to pet the pretty dogs.

They were anything but.

Not only had they died weeks ago, but when they'd come back together, it had been in a pile, in whatever pit the deputy sheriff had dumped them in.

The yellowy-one had the front leg of the black-and-tan one and the body of the brindle.

They were all like that, their legs just enough different lengths to make their movements awkward.

But they got where they were going. And they remembered who had done this to them.

Like all animals, they went for the soft pieces first—the gut, the tongue—and when Dad's porcupine-quill bustle was in the way, one of them grabbed it in its jaws, pulled it away. Instead of coming untied, it peeled from the muscle.

The regalia wasn't ornament, it was part of him. It was what he'd been growing.

Maybe when he just started out, when he was just an impulse, coming back, all he'd had to go on was that dim shape of what he'd meant to be. No clear lines between what he was wearing and what he was.

He really could have been anything.

What he was, though, it was dead. Again.

When the dogs started dragging this feast deeper into the night to take some time with it, pull muscle from bone and tilt their heads back to help it down their throats, I stepped Dino and me back, closed the door as quietly as I could, pushing with my left hand up high, my right hand pulling on the knob, slowing this down.

It didn't matter.

Mom was already there, sitting at the kitchen, her head ducked down to light a cigarette, her hair a shroud over that process.

"What is it?" she said.

I looked out the door again, at the impossible thing happening out there, and then back to Mom, waiting to mete out punishment for whatever was going on here.

"A moose," I told her, and this stopped her second roll on the lighter's wheel.

She stared at me through her hair.

Had Jannie—we used to call her "Jauntie"—told her the truth of what happened to Dad? Had she been carrying this alone for all these years, promising herself to move us away from the stories, so we would be sure never to hear that one?

I should maybe say that we were down in the flats, here. Not that moose are only on the reservation, but they're for sure not all the way down here where they'd be taller than everything.

It was then that I cued in that I was soaking wet.

Mom had noticed too, was about to say something about it, it looked like, when Dino cut in.

"One two three *four*!" he said.

Mom redirected her attention over to him, then back to me.

"You two are the most amazing things I've ever seen," she said, her cigarette still not lit. "I'm—I'm not sorry, I would do it all over again . . . your dad. Everybody told me to stay away from him, that he'd break my heart. But it was worth it, wasn't it? It was all worth it?"

At which point she was sweeping forward to gather us in her arms, in her robe, in her hair, and I think this is where a lot of Indian stories usually end, with the moon or a deer or a star coming down, making everything whole again.

Those stories were all a long time ago, though.

That was before we all grew up.

~

What finally killed Mom, it wasn't her lungs. It was just being sixty-three years old, and nearly a whole state away from all the girls she was in first and second grade with. If she'd had someone to talk with about the old days, I think she'd have maybe made it a few more years.

If she's sixty-three, that would mean I'm thirty-nine now, yeah. Except she died two years ago already. I'm in my forties, Dino his late thirties.

Mom's not why Dad coming back matters now,

though. Why I'm feeling through it all again.

Why it matters—well.

It's hard to know where to start, exactly. Each thing has one thing before it, so I can go all the way back to when I was twelve again, easy.

So, after that night, we just kept growing up. High school was high school. The reservation wasn't the only place with parking lots to fight in. Mom got a desk job, Dino got checked into the first of his facilities and institutions on the tribe's dime. At some point in there, a girlfriend took me to her uncle's house while he was enlisted overseas. He had all the regalia, and when he didn't come back, she smuggled it out to me.

It's backwards, I know—you're supposed to start dancing, then accumulate your gear item by item, piece by ceremonial piece—but this is how I did it. The first time I looked at myself in a full-length hotel mirror, I felt lake water was rising in my throat.

You can dance that away, though.

You can lower your head, raise your knees, close your eyes, and the world just goes away.

I'm not a champion, can't make a living off what I win, but I get around enough, and there's always odd jobs.

News of Mom passing caught up with me two weeks after the funeral. Evidently, Dino had been taken there.

He'd fidgeted in the front row, I imagine, not sure what was going on.

In movies, after you beat the bad guy, the monster, then all the injuries it inflicted, they heal right up.

That's not how it works in the real world.

Here's one way it can work in the real world: the son you accidentally father at a pow-wow in South Dakota grows into the spitting image of a man you remember sitting in the shallows of a lake that goes forever. Like to remind me what I did, what I'd had to do.

You don't see him constant, this son, this reminder, but you see him a few times every year. At least until word finds you—this time, the day after—of a car rolling out into the tall yellow grass. Rolling faster and faster, slopping burger bags and beer cans up into the sky. My son was dead by the time they all landed.

I showed up at the funeral, most of the family and friends strangers to me, and that night, instead of getting in a fight, I walked out into land I didn't know and smoked a whole pack of cigarettes down to the butts. Just staring at the sky. Interrogating it, I guess.

I'd never smoked—you need your lungs if you dance—but after that night, I kind of understood why Mom always had. It makes you feel like you have some control. You know it's bad for you, but you're doing it on purpose, too. You're breathing that in of your own volition, because you want to.

When you don't have control of anything else, when a car can just go cartwheeling off into the horizon, then to even have just a little bit of control, it can feel good. Especially if you hold that smoke in for a long time, only let it out bit by bit.

But eventually I stood from that first pack, and made my way back to my camper, back to the circuit.

Until I got to thinking about what happened when I was twelve.

Which is why I pulled my truck into Dino's parking lot this morning.

Because I'm family, I can check him out with a signature and proof of ID.

He remembers me, too. After his third grade, nothing really changed for him. Just, it's the rest of us who kept changing. But he still sees me as the twelve-year-old I was, I think. The one who fought the monster for him. For all of us.

On the drive out, I tell him about my son. How, if he'd been able to make it through that wreck, how he was going to have taken over the world, Indian-style. Maybe he'd have been a male model, maybe he'd have played basketball, or maybe he'd have been an architect.

Just—that was all gone now.

Unless, right?

When we pull up to the old rent-house, there's nothing there, of course. Instead of dogs in the neighbor's long yard, there's goats behind the chainlink now. They stare at us, never stop chewing.

The house burned down years ago—again, not from cigarettes—but what's still standing, what I wasn't expecting even a little bit, it's the tetherball pole.

There's no ball, no string. But even that it's just still there, it means this can work.

Once, years ago, in the old-time Indian days, a father died, but then he came back. He was different when he came back, he was hungry, he was selfish, but that's just because he already had all that inside him when he died, I know. It's because he carried it with him into the lake that night.

My son—I won't say his name out loud yet—all he would have taken with him, it's his smile, and everything he could have been.

So what we do, it's wait until dark, and walk into the burned pad where the house used to be. The cinderblock pylons are still there, holding up my memory of the floor plan.

I settle us down under what was Mom's bedroom.

Something happened here once, see.

A cat or a possum or a rabbit, it crawled into this darkness to die. But because it was hurt, that gave something else access to it.

Under the tarp in the bed of my truck is all the road-kill I could scrape up, to be turned into body mass, and in raccoon traps at the front of the bed are four hissing cats.

They're not hurt, yet.

There's four because four's the Indian number.

But that's all later.

Right now, I'm just sitting across from Dino. Waiting for him to remember. Is there the least amount of blood seeping down from behind his ear, from where a razor-blade might have traced a delicate X?

There is.

He turned his head to the side for me to do it, like he knew this part already, and I almost couldn't press that metal into his skin.

Almost.

Before him in the dead grass I've set four action figures.

One of them—one of them, I know its life cycle. That morning after, it showed back up on Dino's dresser in his bedroom. Because Mom had found it floating in the dishwater.

It was the only artifact from then. Except for Dino himself.

And now, if he picks that one up instead of the other

three, now they'll be together again, and it can all start all over.

Except—like I say, I know the life cycle, here.

What's going to happen, I know, is that Dino's going to pick up the superhero, not any of the other action figures, and then, because this is part of it, I'll force the left leg into his mouth as gently as I can, as gently as any big brother's ever done a thing like this, and then I'll come up under his chin with the heel of my hand once, fast, so he can bite that foot off.

Maybe he'll swallow it on his own, maybe he'll need help, I don't know.

We've got all night, I mean. He can sit there trying to figure this out and I can dance softly around him in my regalia for as long as it takes, chanting the numbers up to twelve, to prime him, to remind him, the balls of my moccasin feet padding into the dirt over and over in the old way, to wake anything sleeping down there. Anything that can help us get through this ceremony.

And, for my son—*Collin*, Collin Collin Collin—for him to get as solid as he needs to go out into the world like he was supposed to, he's going to need the same thing Dad needed, the same thing Dad got with the neighbor's corpse, the same thing seeping down the side of Dino's neck already.

When will the facility miss him?

It doesn't matter.

They'll never find us way out here, at an address that doesn't exist anymore.

It's kind of like we never even left, really.

I can see the old walls rising around us. I can see the shadow of the roof, the way it was.

When I was twelve years old, I mapped the interior of our home.

Now, sitting across from my little brother, I'm sketching out a map of the human heart, I guess.

There's more dark hallways than I knew.

Rooms I thought I'd never have to enter.

But I will.

For him, for Collin, I'll walk in and pull the door shut behind me, never come back out.

About the Author

STEPHEN GRAHAM JONES is the author of sixteen novels, six story collections, more than two hundred and fifty stories, and has some comic books in the works. His current book is the werewolf novel *Mongrels*. Stephen's been the recipient of an NEA Fellowship in Fiction, the Texas Institute of Letters Jesse H. Jones Award for Best Work of Fiction, the Independent Publishers Award for Multicultural Fiction, three This Is Horror Awards, and he's made Bloody Disgusting's Top Ten Horror Novels of the Year. Stephen teaches in the MFA programs at University of Colorado at Boulder and University of California Riverside–Palm Desert. He lives in Boulder, Colorado, with his wife, two children, and too many old trucks.

TOR·COM

Science fiction. Fantasy. The universe.

And related subjects.

*

More than just a publisher's website, *Tor.com*
is a venue for **original fiction, comics,** and
discussion of the entire field of SF and fantasy,
in all media and from all sources. Visit our site
today—and join the conversation yourself.